Bantam Books in the Choose Your Own Adventure® series
Ask your bookseller for the books you have missed

MAGIC MASTER

BY EDWARD PACKARD

ILLUSTRATED BY FRANK BOLLE

BANTAM BOOKS
NEW YORK • TORONTO • LONDON • SYDNEY • AUCKLAND

RL 4, age 10 and up

MAGIC MASTER

A Bantam Book / March 1992

*CHOOSE YOUR OWN ADVENTURE® is a registered trademark
of Bantam Books, a division of Bantam Doubleday Dell Publishing
Group, Inc. Registered in U.S. Patent and Trademark Office
and elsewhere.*

Original conception of Edward Packard

*Cover art by James Warhola
Interior illustrations by Frank Bolle*

ISBN 0-553-29606-X

Published simultaneously in the United States and Canada

*Bantam Books are published by Bantam Books, a division of Bantam
Doubleday Dell Publishing Group, Inc. Its trademark, consisting of
the words "Bantam Books" and the portrayal of a rooster, is Regis-
tered in U.S. Patent and Trademark Office and in other countries.
Marca Registrada. Bantam Books, 666 Fifth Avenue, New York, New
York 10103.*

PRINTED IN THE UNITED STATES OF AMERICA

OPM   0 9 8 7 6 5 4 3 2 1

MAGIC MASTER

WARNING!!!

Do not read this book straight through from beginning to end. These pages contain many different adventures that you may have when Bonza, the Magic Master, moves to your hometown.

From time to time as you read along, you'll have a chance to make a choice. After you make your decision, follow the instructions to find out what happens to you next.

The amazing Bonza can perform feats of magic unlike any you have ever seen. If you make the right choices, you'll learn the Magic Master's secrets and have a lot of fun. But always think carefully before you act. Otherwise the magician's next trick may be on you.

Good luck!

For a long time you've been wanting to see a performance by the Great Bonza, a world-famous magician who is known as the Magic Master. When your friend Jeff Latham calls to tell you that Bonza has moved to Lakeville, your hometown, you can't help but be excited.

"Are you *sure*? That's pretty hard to believe," you say.

"It's true," Jeff replies. "He bought that big old house with the high hedges on Chestnut Street. My dad's getting us tickets to see Bonza's show in Park City next month. Do you want to come with us?"

"I sure do," you say. "I can't wait!"

Three weeks later, you're sitting in the Memorial Theater in Park City with Jeff and his parents. The lights have dimmed. As you and the rest of the audience wait with anticipation for the show to begin, you see a dog step out from behind the curtain. The dog, a Dalmatian, starts walking slowly across the stage.

An angry voice calls from offstage, "Spot, come back here!"

The dog pauses for a second and looks back, then keeps on walking. A moment later Bonza appears on stage. He is fat and rather silly looking, with a full white beard and a flowing black cape. He's holding a leash, and as he runs stiffly after the dog, he shouts, "Spot, come back! The show hasn't even started yet!"

Turn to page 2.

Everyone in the audience is laughing. You know that they're all wondering the same thing you are: can this goof really be the Great Bonza, the Magic Master?

Suddenly, with a blinding flash of light, the dog disappears!

The audience gasps.

Bonza looks as startled as anyone. He throws up his hands and looks out at the audience sadly. "How can I do my show if my dog has disappeared?" he exclaims.

People start clapping. They realize that Bonza has already performed his first trick.

But Bonza keeps standing there, sad-faced. "I'm not kidding," he says. "That dog is important to me. And now he's gone!"

Bonza sounds so convincing that you're not sure whether to take him seriously or not.

"If only Spot would reappear, I'd be so happy," the magician says. "He was the best dog I ever had."

Suddenly there is a loud bark from the rear of the auditorium. Several people shout, "There he is!" as the dog races up the aisle. He leaps onto the stage and into Bonza's arms.

The audience claps wildly. People shake their heads in amazement. Bonza gives Spot a dog biscuit and a pat on the rump as the dog runs offstage.

Go on to the next page.

After that, Bonza performs one great feat of magic after another, ending with the most amazing trick of all. A curtain is drawn back, revealing Bonza sitting on a horse. The horse is standing on a large wooden platform, which is suspended from the ceiling by four thick chains. A machine makes the platform rise to a height of about six feet above the stage. Bonza, still on horseback, waves at the audience. The curtain is drawn in front of the platform again so the audience can no longer see the horse and rider. Suddenly the curtain and the platform collapse and crash to the floor. The horse and rider have completely disappeared!

Go on to the next page.

The audience gasps in disbelief.

Then, strangely, nothing happens. People begin to get restless.

The manager comes onstage, and the audience quiets down. "I'm terribly sorry," the manager says. "The great Bonza and his horse truly have disappeared. We've called the police and I only hope they can find him. Now I'm afraid I'll just have to ask you to go home."

You follow Jeff and his parents as they file out of the auditorium. When you reach the lobby, there's Bonza, still on his horse, leaning down and signing programs that his fans are holding up to him.

"No wonder they call him the Magic Master," Mr. Latham says.

Turn to page 22.

PARK CITY'S
MEMORIAL THEATER
presents
THE
GREAT
BONZA

The ceiling is so low that it's impossible to stand upright. You crawl cautiously over the straw floor on your hands and knees. Almost immediately your hand touches a rough cinder block wall.

"I just hit a wall," Jeff calls out of the darkness.

"So did I," you say. "You feel along your wall, and I'll feel along mine."

"Okay."

You crawl along the wall, feeling along it every inch of the way. You've only gone a few feet when you touch wood instead of cement. You push it. A tiny wooden door swings open, and bright light pours through, almost blinding you.

You gasp and then cheer. The light is sunlight. The door opens out into Bonza's backyard.

You crawl through and then hold the door until Jeff gets there. The two of you run around the house and race through the opening in the high hedge, hardly stopping to breathe until you're safely out on the sidewalk.

Then Jeff stops and looks at you. "I've had enough of the Great Bonza for a while," he says with a shudder.

"Me, too," you reply. "From now on I think I'll watch his magic shows from a good safe distance."

The End

The two of you circle through the woods and come out at the back of Bonza's property, just behind the barn.

"There's a window on this side, but it's awfully high," Jeff says.

"Boost me up and I'll look in," you say.

"Okay." Jeff bends over so that you can climb up on his back. You peer through the dirty glass. "There's a couple of horse stalls in there," you whisper. "That's all I can see."

"That must be where he keeps the horses he uses in his act," Jeff says. "Let's try to find another way in. He must have something more interesting than horses in there."

Turn to page 90.

Jeff agrees with your plan to ask Bonza to take you on as his assistants. The two of you bike over to Chestnut Street, where Bonza lives.

When you arrive, you peer through a narrow opening in the high hedges at Bonza's Victorian house. It is an impressive-looking structure, with steep-pitched gables, several balconies with vine-covered railings, and a high turret of the sort you might see on a castle. Behind the house to one side, where you'd expect to see a garage, is a large barn.

"It would be fun to see the view from that turret," Jeff says.

"The whole house looks like fun," you reply. "Let's go!"

The two of you park your bikes just inside the hedge and head down the walk toward the front door.

Jeff rings the doorbell several times, but no one answers.

You put your hand on the doorknob and, without thinking, turn it. "Hey, it's unlocked." You push open the door and call out, "Hello, anyone home?" You listen for a moment, but there is no answer. "I guess he's not here," you say. "I'm surprised he'd leave the place unlocked. He must have a lot of valuable things inside."

You start to shut the door again. But Jeff's hand is on your arm. Almost in a whisper he says, "This could be our chance. Let's go in and take a look around. I'm dying to see what kind of stuff he's got in there."

Turn to page 40.

10

"Maybe so," you say under your breath. "But I don't see what good it can do him. He hasn't gotten near the telephone."

Bonza returns to his chair. "Sorry about that," he says. "Now I promise not to get out of the chair again until after you talk to Ralph."

You dial the number. After a few rings someone answers. You keep an eye on Bonza, making sure he's not up to any tricks. "Is Ralph there?" you ask.

"This is Ralph."

Bonza is still sitting motionless, his mouth tightly closed.

"Hi," you say. "My friend and I are over at the Great Bonza's, and he says you have ESP."

"That's right," Ralph says. "I can't explain how it works, but I do."

"Well, then," you say, "I guess you can tell me what card I'm holding right now." You cup your hand over the mouthpiece. If Bonza whispers anything you don't want Ralph to hear it.

"I'm having a little trouble," Ralph says. "Could you concentrate a little harder on the card?"

"Okay," you say. You concentrate on the card you're holding.

Go on to the next page.

"Oh sure, I got it now," says Ralph. "The six of clubs."

"You're right," you say. "That's amazing."

"No problem," says Ralph. "I've got to run. It was nice talking to you."

The phone clicks as Ralph hangs up. "Did I hear you say he got it?" Bonza asks.

"Yeah, he did," you say. "But I don't understand it." You glance at Jeff, but he looks as baffled as you feel.

Turn to page 34.

You and Jeff enter the house and walk cautiously through the darkened hallway and into the living room. The curtains are drawn, and though it's a sunny day, the room is dark and dreary.

"It looks pretty much like a normal living room," Jeff says.

You hardly hear him. You are staring at a painting on the wall. It's a portrait of a man, and his eyes look so real that they seem to follow you as you walk around the room. You wonder if it's possible that Bonza is behind the painting, watching you. You nudge Jeff and say in a low voice, "Maybe we should get out of here."

"Shhssh!" he says, putting a finger to his lips. "We'd better whisper—for all we know there might be someone upstairs. Let's check out the next room."

Turn to page 27.

The page now reads:

YOU HAVE TRESPASSED IN THIS HOUSE,
TAMPERED WITH PROPERTY, AND CAUSED
DAMAGE. LEAVE IMMEDIATELY AND NEVER COME
BACK, OR YOU WILL BE ARRESTED.

You carefully replace the book on the shelf. Then the two of you make a beeline for the door. Neither of you says a word until you pass between the high hedges and reach the street. There's not much use talking about what happened. It's obvious that you're not about to learn the secrets of Bonza, the Magic Master.

The next day at school you describe the book to your science teacher. "How could such a thing happen?" you ask.

"Chemicals," he says. "Though I don't know exactly which ones. The ink in the first message would have to be made of a chemical that fades when it's exposed to light. The second message would be written with an ink that only shows up when it's exposed to light."

Well, you think, at least I learned *one* of Bonza's tricks.

The End

"Forget the book. Let's look in the next room," you whisper.

You and Jeff peer through the door into what seems to be a storeroom. It's filled with lumber and woodworking equipment, drills, sawhorses, cabinets and wooden boxes, black velvet curtains, mirrors, ropes, pulleys, glass balls, bottles, wire cables, film projectors, and all sorts of other odd things. A shaft of sunlight shining through a skylight lights up dust particles suspended in the air.

"Let's look in there," you say, pointing to a large cabinet in the middle of the room. "I bet it has all kinds of secret compartments and stuff."

Jeff has already started toward the cabinet. Suddenly he stops in his tracks and points to a doorway in the opposite wall. You join him and look into the room beyond the doorway. It's dark except for a floodlight on the ceiling, which is trained on a high table in the middle of the room. Sitting on the table is the largest cat you've ever seen. It's at least as big as a medium-sized dog. Its coal black fur is standing on end as if raised by static electricity. Its slanted green eyes seem to give off a light of their own.

"Wow," says Jeff, "that's some cat."

The animal's head moves. Its glowing eyes fix on you like a pair of spotlights. You back up a couple of steps.

"I wouldn't want that thing to jump on me," you say.

Turn to page 39.

Jeff whispers, "I bet he had them up his sleeve."

Hearing him, Bonza shakes his sleeves. "I *never* keep anything up my sleeve." He folds his hands primly in front of himself.

Suddenly a canary pops out from under one of his sleeves. Bonza pretends to look startled. "Oops, guess I was wrong!" He gets up and puts the canary in a cage on the other side of the room. When he comes back, he's holding out the deck of cards. "Take a look through it—make sure it's okay," he says, handing you the deck.

You riffle through the deck of cards as Jeff looks on over your shoulder. "I bet the cards are marked," Jeff says.

"The cards aren't marked," Bonza says, "but it wouldn't matter if they were. My assistant wouldn't be able to see any kind of marking over the phone. Pick a card, any card."

You pull out the six of clubs.

"Okay," says Bonza. "Now we'll phone my assistant, Ralph, and you'll see that he really does have ESP."

"Wait a minute. Where is this assistant of yours?" Jeff demands. "How do we know he isn't hiding behind that portrait on the wall?"

Bonza turns around and looks up at the portrait. "Do you like that? It's a portrait of Harry Houdini, the greatest magician who ever lived."

"The eyes look kind of strange. They're different from a normal painting," Jeff says.

Turn to page 30.

Bonza smiles mysteriously. "That's a secret," he says. He gets up and gestures for you to follow him toward the door. "I thank you for your interest—I'm glad you both stopped by. If either of you ever figures out how Ralph knew which card you were holding, come back. Then if you're still interested, I'll hire you as a magician's assistant."

As you and Jeff walk home, you realize that maybe you don't have what it takes to follow in the footsteps of the Magic Master.

The End

A couple of days later, as you're sitting down to dinner with your parents, your dad says, "Your mom and I got an interesting call last night from a man named Mr. Kramer. He's the lawyer who's representing the Great Bonza."

"I guess he's against Mr. Stafford then," you say.

"That's right," says your dad. "Mr. Kramer wanted to know if you'd be willing to testify in court. He wants you to help prove that the Great Bonza isn't doing anything harmful or illegal in his house and that there's no reason for the neighbors to say he's a nuisance."

"Gosh," you say. "Should I do it?" You look first at your dad and then at your mom.

Your mom says, "I'm sure it would be educational, but going through a trial is bound to be a big hassle. It could also be pretty unpleasant for you to be caught in the middle of this kind of problem. A lot of people in this town support the Concerned Citizens Group. Your father and I are going to leave the decision up to you, but we want you to think carefully about what you're going to do."

Your decision is more difficult than you expected.

If you decide to testify in court,
turn to page 57.

If you decide against it, turn to page 68.

"The explanation," you say, "is that Ralph really does have ESP."

Bonza leans forward in his chair, his hands folded in front of him. "I'm afraid you're wrong," he says. "Ralph doesn't have ESP. In fact, I personally doubt that *anyone* has ESP, although I can't prove it for sure."

"You mean it really was just a magic trick?" Jeff asks.

The Great Bonza nods. "That's right, and I hope you enjoyed it. Now I must ask you two to excuse me. I've got a lot of work to do." He gets up and leads you to the door. "I thank you for your interest, but I'm afraid I can't hire either of you as an assistant."

You and Jeff follow him, feeling rather downcast. When you reach the door, you turn and say, "Well, thanks anyway for showing us some tricks."

"My pleasure," says Bonza. Suddenly four tickets appear in his hand. He gives two to each of you. "Free passes to my next show," he says, smiling. "Come and bring a couple of friends."

The End

On the way home from the show, you and Jeff decide that you're going to find out how the Great Bonza performs his amazing feats.

Mr. Latham, who is driving, overhears your conversation. "Before you get involved with Bonza," he says, "you should know that he's already annoyed a lot of people. His house is in a quiet, residential neighborhood, but he's moved all kinds of equipment into it, and into his barn, too. Some of his neighbors have formed something called the Concerned Citizens Group. They claim that he's a public nuisance. They say they hear strange noises coming from Bonza's barn, and that he sets all the dogs in the neighborhood howling. In fact, some people want to make Bonza move out of Lakeville. They say he's a bad influence on the youth of the community."

"Well, I don't know about that," Jeff says. "But I'd love to find out how he does his tricks."

"Me, too," you say. "Maybe we could get jobs working for him as magician's apprentices."

"Maybe," Jeff says, "but even if we did, I bet it would be a long time before he'd let us in on his really big secrets." He whispers to you, "Maybe we could spy on him."

Go on to the next page.

You grin at the thought. "Let's meet tomorrow after school. Then we'll decide what to do."

The next afternoon, you and Jeff meet at Sam's Soda Shop to discuss your strategy.

If you say, "Let's ask Bonza to hire us as apprentices," turn to page 8.

If you say, "Let's spy on Bonza and see what we can learn that way," turn to page 78.

The next week you return to Bonza's house at nine in the morning, with the agreement that you will work at your new job for three hours every Saturday.

He takes you to a workshop on the other side of the house. It's jammed with electric tools, workbenches, lumber, wires, batteries, and strange-looking electronic equipment.

"This looks like some kind of factory," you say.

"I have an even bigger workshop in the barn," Bonza says. "To be a magician you need a lot of equipment. You have to be a carpenter, a plumber, an electrician, a tailor . . . all sorts of things."

Your first job for Bonza is helping him to build a cabinet with a false bottom. He gives you some tips on how to make furniture, and you both get to work.

After working for a couple of hours, you need a rest. You put down your hammer and go over to watch Bonza, who is placing a piece of coral into a fish tank.

"This is for my disappearing fish trick," he says. "The coral I just put in the tank is hollow. Inside is a miniature projector that projects a hologram of a fish inside the tank. I can make the fish disappear by turning off the projector with a remote control. Of course, the lighting must be just right and the projector aimed at just the right angle for the trick to work and be convincing."

"Wow! Before you get back to work, could you teach me a trick I could do on my own?" you ask.

Turn to page 55.

"That's neat," you say. "I can't wait to learn it."

"It's not hard," Bonza says, "but like most magic tricks, it takes practice."

You and Bonza go back to work. By quitting time the cabinet you're building is almost finished.

"Good work," Bonza says. "Next week I'll show you another trick."

"Sounds good," you say. "I hope someday you'll teach me some of those big tricks—like making a horse disappear!"

Bonza laughs. "I can't tell you my really big secrets. At least not until you're a full-fledged magician."

"When will that be?"

Bonza scratches his chin through his fuzzy white beard. "You have to prove you're dedicated," he says.

"Dedicated? What do you mean?"

"You have to prove that you really want to be a magician."

After you say good-bye to Bonza, you walk down the sidewalk and through the opening in the high hedge in front of his house. You're surprised to see ten or twelve people marching up and down the sidewalk. They're all carrying signs with slogans such as,

BAN BONZA!
WE DON'T WANT BONZA IN OUR TOWN
BONZA'S MAGIC IS A MENACE.

Turn to page 49.

You and Jeff tiptoe toward the open door at the far end of the room. Your eyes are more accustomed to the dimness now, and you notice a bookshelf against the wall by the door. Some of the books on it are so old that their bindings are crumbling into dust. One of them in particular catches your eye. It's a thick volume bound in dark red leather. Printed in gold script on the spine is the title *Secrets of the Great Magicians*.

"Hey, Jeff," you whisper. "Look at this."

"Boy, I bet there's some good stuff in here. Maybe we should take a look," Jeff says.

You glance around the room. Bonza may return any minute now. You want to look at the book, but perhaps you should explore the rest of the house and come back to the volume later if you have time.

*If you decide to look in the book,
turn to page 37.*

*If you decide to look in the next room,
turn to page 15.*

"I want to get a closer look at that cat," you tell Jeff. You step boldly through the doorway. "Good kitty, good kitty," you say. If this cat's real, you want to make sure it's in a good mood.

The cat stares at you curiously for a moment, then starts to purr. Its purr is as loud as its size is big.

"It *is* real," Jeff says. The two of you take another step forward, when suddenly the floor slides out from under your feet. You fall through a trapdoor and land with a thud on a pile of straw below. The door slides shut above you.

You have no idea where you've just landed—it's pitch dark. "You okay?" you ask Jeff.

"Yeah—we only fell about three feet. But now what?" He kneels and pushes against the trapdoor over your heads. "It's locked," he says. "Looks like we're trapped."

"Maybe we'll be able to find another way out once our eyes get used to the dark," you say.

As you sit in the straw waiting for your eyes to adjust, you can feel yourself shaking, wondering if you're trapped for good. For all you know, Bonza may have gone away on a tour. You could starve to death before he returns!

"I still can't see anything," Jeff says after a while.

"Neither can I," you say. "We'll just have to crawl around and see if we can find a way out."

"Okay," Jeff says. "Take it real slow. There's no telling what we might run into here."

Turn to page 6.

Bonza, still looking at the portrait, laughs. "Of course the eyes look different. Houdini wasn't an ordinary man. Why should he have ordinary eyes?" He turns back to you and Jeff. "Oh, wouldn't it be nice if Ralph were willing to hide behind a portrait all day, hoping someone would come along and pick a card?" He points at Jeff. "No, you're wrong, young fellow. Ralph doesn't even live in this town, much less in this house. He lives over in Park City."

Jeff frowns, looking puzzled. "Okay, go ahead and call him then."

"Wait a minute," you say. "How do we know you won't whisper something over the phone? *I'll* call him."

"Fine," says Bonza. He writes Ralph's number down on a piece of paper and hands it to you. "There's the phone, over on my desk. By the way, since it's a long-distance number, you have to dial 1 before the area code."

"All right," you say. "But stay in that chair while I'm calling him, okay?"

"And don't look at the portrait," Jeff puts in.

Go on to the next page.

Bonza laughs. "Sure, sure. Whatever you say." He gestures with his hands, and as he does, another canary hops out of his sleeve. This one takes off and starts flying around the room. Bonza chases it all over the place. Finally the bird settles on the upright piano at the other end of the room, and Bonza is able to cup his hands gently around it and take it to the birdcage.

You and Jeff laugh as you watch Bonza's antics. But as the magician snaps the door of the birdcage shut, Jeff says to you, "He's trying to distract us."

Turn to page 10.

"Let's get out of here," you whisper, but Jeff is already several steps ahead of you. The two of you are about halfway down the walk when a voice calls out from behind you.

"Hello! Can I help you?"

You and Jeff stop short, turn around, and look up. Standing on a second-story balcony is the Great Bonza himself! You call up to him, "We were wondering if we could talk to you."

"Sure, I'll be right down," he says.

You turn back toward the front door and gasp. Bonza is already there—it's as if he has instantly transported himself from the upstairs balcony!

Jeff grabs your arm. "I can't believe what I'm seeing," he says.

You can't believe it either. Bonza seems to be an even greater magician than you'd thought.

You'd probably feel a little scared if Bonza didn't have such a jolly smile on his face. He reminds you a little of Santa Claus, even though he's dressed in black instead of bright red.

When you reach the front step, Bonza says, "Thanks for having the courtesy not to disturb my property. What can I do for you? I'm happy to be of service."

"Thanks," Jeff says.

You introduce yourself and say, "My friend Jeff here and I saw your show in Park City the other evening and we thought it was really great."

Turn to page 47.

"Well, just as I told you," Bonza says. "Ralph's got ESP."

"I'm not sure I believe in ESP," you say.

Bonza's eyebrows go up. "Oh really? Well, maybe you're right," he says. "Just because I say it's so doesn't make it so."

"*Am* I right?" you ask. "It's a trick, isn't it?"

"If you want to be my assistant," Bonza says, "you'll have to tell *me*. Now, I have a horse in the barn I have to tend to. I'll be back in a few minutes. Then I'll see what you two have to say."

Bonza walks out of the room, leaving you and Jeff staring blankly at each other.

"Do you have any ideas?" Jeff asks. "I'm stumped."

"Let me think," you say. You close your eyes, trying to concentrate. By the time Bonza comes back, you have come up with three theories about how Ralph knew what card you were holding. One is that Ralph knows that whenever he's called, the card is the six of clubs. Another idea is that the number you were dialing belongs to a telephone right in this house—maybe behind the portrait of the Great Houdini. The third idea is that Bonza is telling the truth, and Ralph actually *does* have ESP.

Go on to the next page.

"Well," Bonza says, returning to the room and looking straight at you. "Do you have an explanation for me?"

If you say that Ralph knows that when he's called, the card is always the six of clubs,
turn to page 44.

If you say that Ralph is here in this house, probably behind the portrait of Houdini,
turn to page 41.

If you say that Ralph really does have ESP,
turn to page 20.

"Let's see what's in the book," you say. Jeff starts to pull it down. "Careful," you say. "Don't touch the ones next to it. They look as if they might fall apart if you even breathe on them."

Jeff sits down on the floor and opens the book to the first page. You kneel beside him and read over his shoulder:

CHAPTER ONE
THE GREAT MAGICIANS HAVE THREE BASIC
SECRETS THAT GIVE THEM THEIR POWER. THE
FIRST OF THESE IS . . .

Jeff gives a little gasp and whispers, "What's going on? It's fading out."

Go on to the next page.

"This is terrible!" you say out loud, forgetting to whisper.

"We're in trouble now," Jeff says. "I didn't mean to damage any property."

"Wait, look," you say. "The writing is coming back!"

The writing slowly becomes clearer, until finally you can make it out. However, the words are different now from the ones that you saw before!

You and you have trespassed in this house, tampered with property, and caused damage. Leave immediately and never come back, or you will be arrested.

Turn to page 14.

Jeff grabs your arm. "It can't be real," he says. "Cats just don't come that big."

"Maybe it's a hologram," you say, staring back at the huge cat.

"We've got to get closer to tell for sure." Jeff steps across the threshold and then stops short as a voice from within the room says:

"Beware. Turn back. Leave this house immediately."

"That's Bonza," Jeff says. "I recognize his voice from the show we saw."

"I can't tell where it's coming from," you say.

The two of you peer into the corners of the room, trying to see if Bonza is hiding in the darkness.

"It's probably just a recording," Jeff says. "But this place is getting a little too weird for me. Maybe we should get out of here."

If you agree, turn to page 46.

If you decide to stay and find out if the cat is real, turn to page 29.

You don't know what to think of Jeff's suggestion. You're more curious than ever to see the inside of Bonza's house, but you're worried about what could happen if you were caught snooping. "I don't know," you say. "We could get in trouble."

"What trouble?" Jeff says. "We won't take anything. We'll just look around. Chances are no one will ever know. But even if Bonza catches us, what's he going to do? He'll just kick us out and start locking his doors when he's not home."

"He might call the police," you say.

Jeff shrugs. "So he might call the cops, so what? They're not going to put us in jail just for being curious."

You are tempted to look around inside. On the other hand, you have a feeling it might not be a good idea.

If you go inside the house and look around, turn to page 13.

If you decide against it, turn to page 32.

"The explanation," you say, "is that the phone is rigged so that it's connected to where Ralph is perched behind the painting of Houdini. Ralph is hiding there, and he can spy on us through the eyes in the portrait."

"Well, that's an ingenious idea," Bonza says. "I could have hooked a telephone line directly to a space of some sort behind the painting, but you wouldn't have had to dial 1 and then the Park City area code to use it."

"You might have some kind of special arrangement with the phone company," Jeff says.

Bonza chuckles. "Well then, if you don't believe me, go up and touch the portrait's eyes."

You'd had the same idea yourself, and you cross the room eagerly. Standing on tiptoe, you can just reach the top of Houdini's head. You run your fingers across the eyes. They're definitely painted, and there are no cracks in the paint. There's no way those eyes could open.

As you walk back across the room, Bonza says, "No, I give you my word Ralph wasn't behind the painting, or anywhere else where he could spy on us."

"Then how does the trick work?" you ask.

Turn to page 18.

You look at Bonza skeptically. "Are you *sure* it's not up your sleeve?"

Bonza laughs. "Come to think of it, if the glass *had* gone up one of my sleeves, the water would have splashed and the cuff would be wet, right?"

"Right," you agree.

"Feel them."

You run your thumb and forefinger all the way around each of Bonza's shirt cuffs. They're both perfectly dry.

"That's great!" you say.

"Thank you," says Bonza, with a little bow. "And now, since you're a magician's assistant, I'll show you how it's done."

Bonza takes off his jacket and holds it so you can see the lining. Tucked in the back is the missing glass. In the glass is a little rubber ball, just big enough to act as a stopper. At the top of the ball is a tiny screw eye which is connected by an elastic thread to a safety pin attached to Bonza's jacket.

Bonza pulls on the glass, and the thread stretches enough so he can put the glass on the table. He then pulls the ball out of the glass—the water is still in it. "Before I do this trick," Bonza says, "I run the thread up through my sleeves and palm the ball. When I'm ready to do the trick, I press the ball into the glass until it's stuck. When I let go of the ball, the elastic thread pulls it *and* the glass back through my sleeve and around to my back. The ball acts as a cork and holds the water in. That's why my shirt cuffs didn't get wet."

Turn to page 26.

"I bet Ralph knew when I called him that I was holding the six of clubs," you say.

"How would he know?" Bonza demands.

"I gave him a clue of some kind."

Bonza raises an eyebrow. "But you didn't give him any clue."

"Yes, I did!" you say. "You gave me a number to call and told me to say *Ralph*. That's the code word for the six of clubs!"

Bonza looks perplexed. "I didn't tell you to *say* Ralph, I told you his *name* was Ralph."

"Yes, but if I'd held a different card, you would have told me his name was Pete or Bill or Jack, or whatever."

The Great Bonza gets out of his chair and comes over and shakes your hand. "Very good, my young friend. It's true. The fellow you called is not named Ralph at all. His real name is Scott, but he only answers to Scott if the call is from someone holding the ten of diamonds."

"There are fifty-two cards in the deck—that means Scott must have fifty-two names," you say.

"Exactly," says Bonza, "and that means that if you'd still like to, you can have the job of magician's assistant. I'm sorry I can't hire you, too," he says to Jeff, "but I need someone who thinks on his feet."

"That's okay," Jeff says. But on the way home he looks kind of glum. You cheer him up, however, by promising to tell him everything you learn.

Turn to page 25.

You call Bonza and tell him that you've decided to quit your job. You're afraid he'll be angry, but he only says, "I'm sorry to hear it, but I understand. Not many people really want to become full-fledged magicians. I'm sure that whatever you do in life, you will be successful."

"Thanks," is all you can think of to say.

You feel bad about quitting, but not for long. You soon find plenty of other things to keep you busy.

A few days after you quit working for Bonza, your dad mentions that the Concerned Citizens Group has filed a lawsuit against the magician. "Just as I thought," he says. "They're trying to force Bonza to move away."

Turn to page 19.

46

"I think you're right," you say, leading the way out of the workshop.

Walking through the living room, you pass the bookcase with the book titled *Secrets of the Great Magicians.* This may be your last chance to take a look at it.

If you stop to look at the book,
turn to page 37.

If you say, "Let's get out of here,"
turn to page 32.

"Well, good," says Bonza, looking more jolly than ever.

Jeff edges in front of you. "We were wondering if you could tell us how you do those tricks."

Bonza's eyebrows go up. "You think they're just tricks? You don't believe in true magic? Well don't be so sure. Besides, if there were a trick to it, and I told you, you wouldn't have the fun of not knowing."

"Hmmm," you say, trying to think of what to say next. Finally you grin at him. "That's okay, tell us anyway."

Bonza shakes his head. "Magicians never give away their secrets. The only way for you to find out is to become magicians yourselves."

"We'd like that," you say. "We were hoping we could become your assistants."

"Ah," says Bonza. "Then come on in." He leads you into his darkened living room and asks you and Jeff to sit on the sofa. Then he pulls up a chair to face you.

"I'd be glad to take you on," he says. "But only if you can prove that you'd be better than my present assistant. I should warn you, though, that may be a tough job for you. He has ESP."

"You mean extrasensory perception?" you say.

"That's right. If you pick a card and then telephone him, he can tell you what card it is over the phone."

"I don't believe it," Jeff says.

A deck of cards suddenly appears in Bonza's hand.

Turn to page 16.

An angry-looking woman spots you coming through the hedge. "You shouldn't have any dealings with that man!" she shouts.

"You'll get yourself in trouble hanging around Bonza!" someone else yells.

You do your best to ignore the protestors and hurry away.

The following Monday you tell your home-room teacher, Ms. Gillette, about your job with Bonza and about the people picketing outside his house.

"I've read about them in the paper," she says.

"What do you think they're so angry about?"

"I wish I knew! They just seem to be angry because he's so different."

"Gee," you say. "I've learned some of his tricks, and they're really cool. I'll show you some myself."

"You don't have to, I believe you. But don't show any to those people picketing," Ms. Gillette says. "They'd probably think that you're a troublemaker, too."

Turn to page 60.

You explain how you learned different tricks and how to make props for Bonza's shows. You say that there was nothing illegal involved in any of the tricks you saw. You mention that Bonza keeps canaries, dogs, and horses for his act, and that they make some noise, but not any more than the average neighborhood dog. You also say that Bonza takes good care of his animals and is never mean to them.

This part of the trial is easy. Then Mr. Kramer sits down and Mr. Stafford, the lawyer for the Concerned Citizens, stands up.

The judge says, "You may proceed with your cross-examination, Mr. Stafford."

The lawyer walks up close to the witness box and stares at you suspiciously. "So," he says, "you say you learned quite a few magic tricks from the Great Bonza?"

"That's right, sir."

"And you learned how to build props for other tricks."

"Yes, sir."

Mr. Stafford looks over at the jury for a moment; turning back to you, he says, "So, you could put on a pretty good magic show yourself?"

"Well, I think I could, sir, with a little more practice," you say.

Go on to the next page.

"You must be quite talented," says Mr. Stafford. "You're already a young magician!"

You can't help grinning a little. You'd thought Mr. Stafford might be nasty, but instead he's complimenting you.

Mr. Stafford gives you a warm smile. "Am I right?"

Turn to page 112.

"Why should Bonza have to move away?" you demand.

"Because he's a nuisance to the community, and he might cause a lot of harm!"

"Really? I don't see how he could be any harm to anybody."

Stafford wiggles a finger at you. "Don't be so sure. There's something very strange about Bonza—and his tricks."

"But I've seen some of his tricks—I know how they work!"

Stafford shakes his head. "Just as I thought. Bonza has you fooled with all his tricks. You've really been taken in by him. You can't even see what a menace he is to the standards of this fine community. It really is a shame. You seem like a decent kid at heart, if you could just escape from that black-suited troublemaker's treacherous influence!"

"I've got to go," you say, "or I'll miss my bus."

Stafford points toward the waiting school bus. "Go then, but remember: if you want to keep out of trouble, never go near Bonza again!"

Turn to page 65.

You have a lot of trouble sleeping that night. You can't stop worrying about whether or not to keep your job with the Great Bonza. You're curious to learn more, but you must admit that there's something a little odd about Bonza. And you don't want to have half the people in town thinking you're odd, too!

If you decide to keep your job, turn to page 66.

If you decide to quit, turn to page 45.

Bonza grins. "Why not?" He takes off his smock, goes to the closet, and takes out a jacket. Then he shows you a tiny drinking glass, only an inch across and a couple of inches high. He fills it halfway with water from the sink and holds it in front of you. "Now I'm going to make the water in this glass disappear right in front of your eyes."

"I'm watching," you say.

Bonza says, "First I have to get some powder from my back pocket that makes the water disappear." He holds the tiny glass in one hand and with the other reaches around behind him. When he brings his hand back, he seems to pinch something into the glass. Whatever it is, you can't see it, but suddenly not only the water but the whole glass is gone!

"Confound it, I lose more glasses that way!" Bonza cries.

"What happened? Where did it go?" you ask. You're impressed—you were watching carefully. It looked to you as if the glass really *did* disappear into thin air, although you know that there has to be a trick to it.

Turn to page 64.

"Show me how you saw a woman in half," you say.

Bonza beckons you to follow him to the other side of his workshop. "This box goes on the platform you just made. You'll notice that the box is about four feet long, a foot high, and two feet wide. See how the top swings up. The woman lies down in the box with her head sticking out one end and her feet sticking out the other. There are two little doors in the side of the box that faces the audience. I open the doors so that everyone can see her arm through the first door and her leg through the second door. Next I close the doors and the top of the box. Then I saw right through the middle of the box and pull the two halves apart. It's obvious that I've sawed the woman in half."

"But you really haven't, have you?" you inquire.

Turn to page 67.

"Tell Mr. Kramer that I'll testify," you tell your dad.

Two weeks later, you get the day off from school so you can testify in the court case *Concerned Citizens versus the Great Bonza*.

You've seen some court cases on television, but never in real life. The judge, a distinguished-looking man in a long black robe, peers down at you from his chair. The twelve jurors study you from their benches. Mr. Stafford, the lawyer for the Concerned Citizens, glares at you from his table.

Mr. Stafford first calls an expert witness to the stand. The witness, a magician himself, says that Bonza does tricks no magician could possibly do, and that he therefore must be doing something illegal. Then Mr. Stafford calls several of Bonza's neighbors to the stand. They all say that they haven't been able to sleep at night because of the strange noises coming from Bonza's property. They also say that they are always nervous about what kinds of things may be going on over there.

Finally it's your turn to testify. The clerk swears you in.

Mr. Kramer stands up and walks over to question you. He asks you to describe the job you had with Bonza.

Turn to page 50.

Mr. Kramer, the lawyer, pauses for a moment. Then he says softly, "You jury members are smarter than that. You know that just because we can't tell how something is done doesn't mean there's no good explanation for it. The Concerned Citizens have offered no proof that Bonza has been a nuisance, or done anything illegal."

The lawyers are finished. The judge instructs the jury members, and they file out of the room. It takes them only a few minutes to bring back their verdict: "We find the defendant, the Great Bonza, innocent!"

Everyone looks over to where the Great Bonza was sitting, thinking that he will stand up and cheer. To your amazement and that of everyone else, he's no longer there! In his chair are only his magician's cape, his trousers, jacket, belt, socks, and shoes.

Mr. Stafford jumps up, screaming, "That proves it, Your Honor—Bonza is a troublemaker and a threat to our community!"

But as the judge slams his gavel down on his desk, he thunders, "Silence, Mr. Stafford. This case is dismissed!"

The End

As the weeks go by, you gain many new skills, and you learn several magic tricks. But Bonza doesn't seem to have his heart in his work. You suspect that the picketers have something to do with his attitude. They have been protesting outside of his house every day, getting louder and more insulting all the time.

One Saturday, when you're through with your work, he says, "I don't think you'd better come back anymore. People will begin to think you're a troublemaker like me."

"That's ridiculous," you protest.

"Lots of things are ridiculous, but they seem to happen anyway," Bonza says. "Thanks for wanting to stick by me, but I don't want to drag a kid down into my feud."

"Maybe it will all blow over in a few weeks," you say.

Bonza brightens a bit. "Maybe. If so, then you could help me get ready for my next big show."

A few days later, as you're heading for your bus after school, a man comes up to you. He's wearing a pin-striped suit and a tie and is carrying a leather briefcase. "Hi," he says in a friendly voice. "My name is Howard Stafford. I'm a lawyer, representing the Concerned Citizens Group."

"What's that?" you ask.

"It's a group of citizens who believe that the Great Bonza is a bad influence in our community. They've hired me to bring a lawsuit to get him to move out of town."

Turn to page 52.

"The answer, my young friend, is that there are two horses and two riders. You only see the horse and rider onstage for a few seconds. The horses are practically twins, and the rider is dressed to look like me, with a false beard and a cape just like mine. In the dim light, no one can tell the difference. All the time I've been waiting on my horse out in the lobby."

You smile, impressed. Just wait until I tell Jeff, you think to yourself.

After the show, Bonza surprises you by telling you that he's going to retire and move to Florida.

"When are you leaving?" you ask.

"I'm afraid right now," he says. "I've already sold my animals. A woman bought the horses, and she had a van waiting to take them away after the show. The movers are taking all the things out of my house in the middle of the night."

"But why?"

Bonza grins broadly. "So that when the Concerned Citizens come to picket me in the morning, they'll find that I've disappeared."

"But they'll probably think that you took off because you did something wrong," you say.

"I know," Bonza says with a wink. "And they'll probably worry about it for a long time, too."

The End

"Now, if my ESP is working," says Bonza, "you're thinking that the ball could be held up by a thread."

"That's right!" you say. "I *was* thinking that."

"The ball's much too heavy for that," says Bonza, "but don't take my word for it. Watch." He stands a few feet to one side of the silver ball and makes a hoop with his arms, locking his fingers together. Then he walks toward the ball, completely encircling it with his arms, and keeps walking until he's well past it.

You blink. If there had been a thread holding up the ball, his arm would have run against it and set the ball swinging.

"Okay," says Bonza. "It's time for the ball to go back in its closet." He reaches for the ball, but it darts away from him. He reaches again, and again the ball escapes. Finally, with a great lunge, he captures it and carries it offstage.

Turn to page 106.

64

Bonza looks around on the floor and even up at the ceiling, as if the glass might be up there. "I really have trouble with that trick," he says. "I just want to make the water disappear, but then the glass disappears, too!"

"You did an even bigger trick than you planned," you say. At the same time you're trying to figure out what happened. "I bet somehow the glass went up your sleeve," you say.

Bonza's eyebrows shoot up. "You think so?" He shakes his sleeves vigorously. Nothing comes out. "I wish that were the answer," he says. "Then I'd have my glass back."

Turn to page 42.

When you get home, you tell your parents about Mr. Stafford and repeat his warning to you.

"I've heard of Stafford," your dad says. "He's the lawyer for the Concerned Citizens Group. The group is bringing a lawsuit to make the Great Bonza move out of town. They say that he makes a lot of noise, that he's a public nuisance, and that he's corrupting children like you."

"That's stupid," you say. "They can't get away with that, can they?"

"I wouldn't think so," your dad says, "but if they can prove that he's a nuisance to his neighbors, they could order him to stop his activities. It's true that he's got a workshop and keeps animals—he's sort of running a business there—and I'm not sure that's legal in that part of town."

Your mom says, "Your father and I have always felt you should be free to learn about anything you want, as long as it's not immoral or illegal. From what you've told me, there is nothing immoral or illegal in what Bonza does. You've learned a lot about carpentry and electricity and other things and mastered some good magic tricks. I'm beginning to worry, though, that some of the things Bonza does could be dangerous. Also, I'd hate to see you get too mixed up with those people in the Concerned Citizens Group. I'd just be careful, if I were you."

Turn to page 54.

You phone Bonza to tell him that you want to stick with your job despite anything the Concerned Citizens might say.

"I'm glad to hear it," he says. "You've convinced me that you truly want to become a magician. For that reason I want you to help me prepare for my next big show."

"Does that mean I'll learn some of your big secrets?"

"Yes, indeed," Bonza says. "You'll be helping me to prepare the equipment. You'll learn *one* of my big secrets this time, and someday, as you get better at your job, you'll learn them all."

The next Saturday morning, when you go to Bonza's house, there are even more members of the Concerned Citizens Group picketing than before. As you're about to pass through the opening in the hedge, a burly man comes up to you. "Are you going in that house?" he demands, grabbing your arm.

"Yes, I'm going in there. There's no reason I shouldn't," you say.

"Well," says the man, "you tell Bonza that if he goes through with his next show, we'll have to take matters into our own hands."

You twist loose from the man and hurry through the hedge. He shouts after you, "You better warn him—it's for his own good, and yours, too!"

When you get inside the house, Bonza is all smiles. "Ah, I'm glad you're here," he says. "Let's get started. We've got a lot to do."

Turn to page 79.

"Of course not. Like most magic tricks, it's really very simple," Bonza says. "You see, when the woman gets in the box, she pushes two fake feet, molded to look just like hers, through the other end of the box. Then she pulls her legs sideways, so her knees are as close to her chest as possible. She braces her feet against a partition between the two halves of the box. When I open the doors on the side of the box, the people in the audience think they see one of her arms, her side, and one of her legs. Actually the leg is fake, just like the feet. I close the door, and the woman can move her fake feet by pulling on strings. When I saw the box in half, I'm only cutting her off from her fake legs and feet!"

"That's terrific," you say. "And then you fasten the two parts of the boxes together. The woman pulls in the fake feet, and when you open the top of the box, she gets up and waves at the audience!"

"Exactly. It fools them every time," says Bonza. "But only because my regular assistant, Gilda Rossini, and I practice a lot, so we can do the trick just right."

Turn to page 89.

You decide not to testify, and your father calls Mr. Kramer to give him the news.

A week later the local newspaper has a small headline near the bottom of the front page. It says LAWSUIT AGAINST MAGICIAN DROPPED.

For a moment you feel pleased. It sounds as if the Concerned Citizens decided that they didn't have a good case. But as you read on, you feel a lot less happy. The reason the lawsuit has been dropped is that Bonza has decided to leave town anyway. As he told a reporter, "I had hoped that the people of Lakeville would be happy to have me here, but it turns out I was wrong. Having seen magic tricks they don't understand, they automatically assume that I must be doing something illegal, and that I'm a troublemaker."

Then the reporter asked Bonza where he was moving to. He answered, "Someplace where people aren't so narrow-minded."

The End

At that moment you hear a noise from below. You walk to the edge of the loft and look over. A fierce-looking German shepherd has somehow gotten into the workshop. It's pacing back and forth, as if on guard. You watch it sniff at the ladder you just climbed up. It looks up and barks, just once, as if to tell you that it knows you're there.

Jeff joins you, peering down at the dog. "How do you think it got in?"

You point toward a little door across from the stalls where you came in. It was closed before, but now it's standing open. "I bet that when the electric eye went off and started the recording, it also opened the door and let the dog in. Now we're stuck up here. I have a feeling we made a mistake trying to outwit the Great Bonza."

"Should I try the lion's roar now?" Jeff asks.

"No! That won't help," you say once again, giving him an exasperated look to keep his itchy fingers off the sound effects machine.

Go on to the next page.

Suddenly the door from the horse stall opens. You motion to Jeff to duck. The recording starts playing. The dog, who has been looking up the ladder, turns and starts toward the open door. An object goes flying toward the dog, and the door slams shut. You can see that the object is a large piece of beefsteak.

The dog sniffs at it and then drags it off to a corner to chew on. The stall door slowly opens again. You expect to see Bonza enter, but instead you see two men wearing camouflaged hunting gear, each carrying a gun. The dog glances at them but is obviously more interested in the steak than the criminals.

Turn to page 84.

You push the key on the sound effects machine marked LION'S ROAR. You've heard a lion roar in the zoo, but never one as loud as this. The intruders jump about four feet in the air. They rush toward the door they came in. The dog jumps up and runs after them, but they make it through and slam the door in the animal's face. The dog leaps up against the door, growling and barking. You and Jeff start laughing, but you stop in a hurry when the dog runs over to the foot of the ladder and starts barking at you.

"It looks as if we're still stuck here," Jeff says. "And if Bonza finds us up here he'll never believe we prevented a robbery."

A voice rings out from the direction of the horse stalls. "Of course he will." It's the great Bonza! He is standing in the doorway, wearing his magician's cape. The dog runs up to him, wagging its tail. "You two can come down now," Bonza says.

"We can explain," you say as you hop down from the ladder.

"You don't have to," says Bonza. "I heard everything everyone said. It's all on tape." He snaps his fingers at the dog. "Right Rex?" The dog barks once and then suddenly drops to the ground and starts rolling over and over. You wonder if it's gone mad. But Bonza doesn't seem to notice. He says in a casual tone, "Are you two going to say anything about how you just barged in here without permission?"

Turn to page 86.

"Ever since I saw your show in Park City, I've been wondering how you and your horse disappeared from the stage and reappeared in the lobby," you say. "I want to find out how it's done."

"Ah, yes, that's quite a trick, if I do say so myself," says Bonza. "You saw how I was sitting on the horse on a platform suspended by chains. Well, a machine makes the platform rise several feet in the air. I wave at the audience. The curtain is drawn in front of the platform again so the audience can no longer see me or the horse. Then the curtain and platform collapse on the stage, and we've disappeared.

"Here's how that trick is done: After the curtain is drawn, the floor of the platform, with me and the horse standing on it, is slid back through an almost invisible opening in the backdrop and another platform takes its place. The platform and curtain collapse, and there's nothing there. The audience never guesses that the horse and rider are just a few feet behind the backdrop. And before they think any more about it, the manager comes out and says the show is over. Seconds later, people are astounded to see me on my horse, riding around in the lobby."

"But Bonza, how could you get to the lobby so fast? When we saw that trick in Park City, it seemed almost instantaneous."

Turn to page 61.

Bonza motions you through the door and accompanies you out of the barn. "All right, just this one trick," he says. "The mice cage was sitting on a special platform which is hooked up to a silent electric motor. When I push a button on a remote control device, the platform sinks below floor level. You wouldn't think there would be a basement in a barn, and you can't see the stairs going down to it. But there is one, with a lot of machinery. The platform holding the mice cage drops down into the basement, and a section of floor slides into place where it was, so that it looks as if it was never there at all."

Jeff stares at the magician in disbelief. "But you did all this right in front of our eyes, and we didn't even notice!"

Bonza nods. "There wasn't a chance in a million you'd see it happen. You were watching Rex, wondering why he was rolling over."

"Why was he rolling over?" you ask. "You didn't tell him to."

"Ah, but I did," says Bonza. "When I say the word *Right,* Rex rolls—look, he's doing it now!" Bonza points to the dog. Sure enough, Rex is rolling over again. "And when I say *Rex, stop that,* he stops."

You and Jeff shake your heads, smiling.

"Rex is one of my best assistants," Bonza says. "Even if he'd rather eat a steak than chase criminals."

The End

"Objection," Mr. Kramer says.

But before the judge can rule, Mr. Stafford says, "Question withdrawn. No further questions."

The judge tells you to step down.

Everyone starts talking at once.

Bang! Bang! Bang! The judge raps his gavel. "Order in the court."

People quiet down. You sit down in the back of the courtroom while the two lawyers sum up their cases.

Mr. Stafford repeats what he has said before—that Bonza has been disturbing the peace of the neighborhood and generally causing trouble. Practically shouting at the jurors, he finishes by saying, "The Great Bonza is a menace and a nuisance, not only to his neighbors, but to all the people of Lakeville!"

Go on to the next page.

Then Mr. Kramer gets up. He speaks in a calm, unhurried tone. "For something to be a nuisance, it has to be harmful," he says. "Have any of Bonza's tricks been harmful to the people of Lakeville? Some people have been made unhappy, it's true. But that's because of what's been going on in their own minds, not because of anything that the Great Bonza has done." Mr. Kramer walks closer to the jury. He waves a hand toward where Mr. Stafford and the Concerned Citizens are sitting. "These people are upset. Why are they upset? It's not because the Great Bonza is hurting them, but because they can't understand how he does his tricks! They are so stubborn, so arrogant, they think that if someone does something they can't understand, he or she must be doing something wrong."

Turn to page 58.

You decide to spy on Bonza and see if you can learn how he does his tricks. The following Saturday morning you and Jeff walk by the high hedge in front of Bonza's house. There's a narrow opening through which you can see the front door and the house, a large Victorian structure with a tower at the top.

The property is bordered on three sides by a thick hedge which screens the neighboring houses from view. A long driveway on one side of the property leads to a barn behind the house. Beyond the hedge in the back is the forest.

"If we go up the front walk or the driveway, we're likely to be spotted," Jeff points out. "Let's approach from the woods."

"Good idea," you say. "We can come out behind his barn. From what your dad said, it sounds as if he has his workshop there."

Turn to page 7.

You tell Bonza first about the warning the man outside gave you.

Bonza laughs. "Those crazies. What are they going to do—hang me on the village green?" Bonza gives you a grin that changes your mood. Instead of being worried about the Concerned Citizens' threats, you feel like laughing at them.

That day you work on building a platform for one of Bonza's tricks, while Bonza works on a complicated-looking device with pulleys and ropes. By eleven o'clock the platform is finished. Bonza walks around it, bending over to see how the supports rest on the floor. He steps up onto it and jumps up and down. "Good and solid," he says. "Just the way I like it."

"I'm glad," you say. "Is there another job you want me to do?"

"No," Bonza says. "It's time for us to talk about the show. You'll be helping me with two of my biggest tricks. I'll teach you how one of them is done, and I'll let you decide which one it'll be. The first trick is the one where I saw a woman in half without her being hurt; the second trick is the one where I make a horse and rider disappear and then reappear somewhere else."

"I'd like to learn both," you say.

Bonza wiggles a finger at you. "You have to choose one."

If you decide to learn how to saw a woman in half without hurting her, turn to page 56.

If you decide to learn how to make a horse and rider disappear, turn to page 73.

80

You look around the stall. Suddenly you spot a tiny object that looks like a miniature flashlight set in the wall near the stall door. "I wonder if that's an electric eye," you say, pointing it out to Jeff.

"Hey," he says, "if there's no one here to stop us, let's just look around a little more. I want to see what's up in that loft." He points to a ladder that leads up to what must have once been a hay-loft.

You both enter the main room of the barn again and close the door behind you. You half expect the recording to play something more, but all you hear is the chirping of the birds in the cage.

Jeff climbs up the ladder until he can see over the edge. "Hey, this is cool—there's all kinds of equipment up here," he calls down to you. He climbs into the loft.

Turn to page 96.

One day you decide to call Bonza. You tell him about your new magic set and ask him if he's still willing to teach you one of his secrets.

"I'm afraid I can't," he says. "But I'll *tell* you a little secret. Some people have fun learning a little magic. But they don't love magic enough to become a Magic Master. You're one of those people, I can tell. There's nothing wrong with that. Someday you'll want to master some other skill, one that's more important to you. Be on the lookout for it."

You're disappointed that Bonza won't tell you his magic secrets, but you realize that what he says is true. You like magic, but not enough to dedicate your life to it. "Thanks," you say. "Well, so long."

"So long," says Bonza, "and by the way, all through your life, keep an eye out for what's real and what's fake. It really helps to know the difference."

The End

You decide to try to plan a strategy. You notice there's a space between the two front seats. You could twist around, reach forward, and set off your smoke bomb right under the driver's nose. He's still driving fast, and he'd be almost certain to crash. It could be your only chance to escape.

On the other hand, you could be killed in the crash, and if you weren't, the robbers might shoot you in anger. Maybe it would be better to save the smoke bomb until you get to the river. You're a fast runner, and you might be able to blind them with smoke long enough to escape into the woods. You know that both plans are risky, but you can't think of any other way out of this mess.

"That's Bob's Diner ahead," one of the men says.

*If you try your smoke bomb now,
turn to page 94.*

If you decide to wait, turn to page 114.

As the two men look around the barn, you hear one of them say, "So where's all the valuable stuff you told me about? All I see is a bunch of junk."

"You think I'd bring you here to show you a bunch of mice and fish?" the other man replies. "Wait'll you see what's up in the loft—this magician's got even more electronics than that last place we hit."

The first man chuckles. "Sure beats mice." They both start laughing. "Come on, let's go."

The dog looks up from its steak. It gives a low, throaty growl, but then starts eating again.

You turn to Jeff and whisper, "We've got to stop these guys."

He looks at you wide-eyed. "But what can we do?"

You glance at the sound effects machine. "I know what to do," you say.

If you push the key on the machine marked LION'S ROAR, turn to page 72.

If you push the key on the machine marked EARTHQUAKE, turn to page 92.

If you just yell, "STOP!" turn to page 97.

"We're sorry for snooping," Jeff says. "But at least we scared off those criminals."

"I'm sorry too," you say, trying to think of a way to change the subject. "You sure have a lot of neat stuff. Are those the mice you use in your act?"

"Mice? What mice?" Bonza says.

You and Jeff look over at the mice cage. Not only are the mice gone, but the cage that held them is missing! You can hardly believe your eyes.

"What happened to the mice? They were right there!" Jeff exclaims.

Bonza says, "Oh yes, the mice. I guess those two men got away with them."

"They didn't," Jeff says. "They were so scared of the lion, they just ran."

"The mice cage disappeared," you say, "and you *made* it disappear." You point at Bonza.

Bonza looks surprised. "Now how could I have done a thing like that? You're saying the mice disappeared, right?"

Suddenly the dog starts rolling over again.

Bonza says, "*Rex!* Stop that!" Then he turns back to you and says, "Now what makes you think the mice disappeared?"

Go on to the next page.

You look back toward the corner where the mice were—and the cage is back again!

You and Jeff exchange glances. "This is wild," he says.

"Well, you two will have to excuse me now," Bonza says. "I know I have your word you won't sneak back in here without permission."

"Yes, sir," you say, "but before we leave, could you please just tell us how you made the mice disappear and come back?"

Turn to page 75.

The following Saturday is Bonza's big show. You're backstage helping with the props and lighting as he seems to saw a woman in half. Afterward the audience gives him a standing ovation.

Jeff and some of your other friends from school have come to the performance, and you invite them backstage to meet Bonza. After you've introduced them, and he signs autographs, Bonza draws you aside. "That was my last performance," he says. "I'm retiring to Florida."

"Gee, I'm sorry to see you go," you say. "I was hoping to learn a lot more of your tricks."

Bonza laughs. "But of course you will, if you want to be a magician," he says. "You'll learn them from books and from other magicians. And you'll think up new ones on your own." He reaches out to shake your hand, but suddenly a canary appears in it. The little bird takes off, with Bonza right behind it.

You and your friends laugh.

"That's Bonza," you explain. "He can't stop doing tricks."

The End

The two of you continue along the side of the barn and spot a couple of horses grazing in the small meadow behind the house. You peer around the edge of the barn. From where you are standing, you can see that the horse stalls open out into the meadow. "I think we could probably get into the barn through those stalls," you say. "But we'd be within sight of the house for a few seconds, if anyone's looking."

"Let's take a chance," Jeff says.

"Okay." In a flash you're around the corner and into the nearest stall. Jeff follows. You cross over to the door at the back of the stall, keeping an eye where you step. You open the door and peek into the central part of the barn. The sun streams in through two huge skylights in the roof. You see more animals, some of which you recognize from Bonza's performance. There's a glass case in one corner that contains about a dozen white mice, a large aquarium full of all kinds of fish, and a birdcage which is so large that it reaches almost to the rafters. Canaries, parakeets, and parrots perch on the branches of several full-sized trees growing inside the cage.

You step through the stall door. Immediately a loud voice booms, *"You are trespassing. Leave now and don't come back."*

Go on to the next page.

Startled, you look around. There's no one in sight. You cautiously take another step forward.

"This is your last warning," the voice says.

You back up into the doorway, almost running into Jeff, who is right behind you. "Can you tell where it's coming from?" he asks.

"No—it sounds like it's coming out of thin air."

"I bet it *is* coming out of thin air," Jeff says. "It's probably a recording. We must have set it off when we walked through the door."

Turn to page 80.

You slam two fingers down on the EARTHQUAKE key. Then you clap your hands over your ears. The noise is deafening! Tables, chairs, cages, everything shakes. The robbers race for the door, with the German shepherd right behind them.

The noise subsides into a low rumble, but things are still shaking. "Come on," you say to Jeff. "We'd better get out of here. Bonza or the cops could show up any minute."

You and Jeff are down the ladder and out the door in no time. The robbers are nowhere in sight, but Bonza is standing outside the barn with the dog beside him. "You don't need to explain," he says. "I heard you and the robbers talking on a remote speaker. Thanks for chasing them away, even if you had to set off the Earthquake to do it."

Suddenly you hear a siren. A police car is coming up the drive. It screeches to a stop, and two officers jump out.

"What's going on here?" one of the officers says. "We got reports of an explosion. Someone complained there was a rumble like an earthquake."

Bonza grins. "That proves my earthquake machine is realistic," he says. "I thought I still had some bugs to work out."

Turn to page 99.

The following week the newspaper runs a front-page story about the Great Bonza. You read that the judge ordered Bonza to stop using his property as a workshop to build props. "You've made too much noise and frightened the neighbors," the judge ruled.

The lawyer for the town wanted to make Bonza pay a fine, but the judge wouldn't allow it. He said it was enough of a penalty for Bonza to have to move his business elsewhere.

A few weeks later you learn that Bonza has moved. But you'll never forget him, or his wonderful tricks.

The End

You manage to pull the smoke bomb canister out of your pocket.

"Hey, what's that?" the man holding you says, but you've already thrust the can through the space between the two front seats. You take a big gulp of air, close your eyes, and press the red button on top of the can. Instantly the car fills with smoke. The men curse. The car swerves. You brace yourself for a crash. The man holding you coughs violently.

You hear the squealing of tires, then the sound of ripping metal as the car sideswipes another. Your car flips at a ninety-degree angle and careens into the ditch.

The back door flies open. You open your eyes, jump out of the car, and roll into a ditch. Out of the corner of your eye, you see one of the men leap from the backseat and aim his gun. You crouch low and run along the ditch.

Bob's Diner is only a hundred feet down the road. And, you're happy to see, there's a police car parked outside. Two officers rush out. A bullet whistles past your ear. Shots come from the other direction—the police are firing back!

You dive behind a big tree, safe for the moment. The two men have run back to their car and are trying to get away, but the right front wheel is stuck in the ditch.

Turn to page 101.

In a moment you join him. Your eyes fasten on a shelf filled with interesting-looking containers. One of them, a small can with a red button on top, says WARNING: SMOKE BOMB. Beyond the shelf is something that looks like a piano, but the sign on it says SOUND EFFECTS. Each key is labeled with a different sound.

Jeff says, "I want to try this one." He puts a finger above the key labeled LION'S ROAR.

You grab his hand. "Don't! Bonza will hear it for sure."

Another key says EARTHQUAKE. "That would be cool," you say.

Jeff grins at you. "Shall I try it?"

"Don't." You're still worried that someone will hear.

Turn to page 70.

You lean over the edge of the loft and yell, *"Stop!"* Then, as an afterthought, you add, "The police are on their way!"

The robbers jump at the sound of your voice, but then one of them pulls a gun. He calls, "Come down from there—real slow and easy."

Jeff has stayed crouched out of sight. As you get to your feet, you press down on his shoulder, signaling him to stay low. You walk toward the ladder, past the shelf with the can labeled SMOKE BOMB on it. You grab the can and cram it into the pocket of your jacket. Then you climb slowly down the ladder.

"If *we* don't get past the cops, *you* don't get past the cops," the man with the gun says. He prods you along, out the door and across the strip of grass between the barn and the woods. Then he and his friend force you to march through the woods to a dirt road. An old station wagon is parked at the side of the road. One of the men gets behind the wheel and starts the engine as the other one shoves you into the backseat. He holds you down on the floor as the car takes off.

The man holding you shoves a towel in your face, trying to muffle you. But you twist your head and yell, "Where are you taking me?"

"Another word out of you and I'll jam this down your throat!" the man says menacingly.

"We're taking you to where they won't find your body for a long time," the driver adds.

Again you wrest loose from the towel. "Let me go! I won't cause you any trouble!"

Turn to page 107.

"You're the magician everyone's talking about, aren't you?" the police officer says, pointing a finger. "Well, this neighborhood isn't the place for your sound effects. This is a residential area, not an amusement park! I'm going to have to serve you with a summons." He writes out a ticket and hands it to Bonza.

The magician takes the ticket, but suddenly it disappears from his hand. Bonza says, "I thought you were going to give me a summons, officer?"

The cop moves closer. "I'll give you a night in jail, if you don't watch out." As he says this, he starts writing out another summons. He holds it out for Bonza to take. "Don't let this one disappear like the other one, or you'll be in *real* trouble."

Bonza starts to reach out for the ticket, but suddenly the missing one is back in his hand!

The officer glares at him.

Bonza says, "Officer, the summons didn't disappear. Here it is."

The officers can't help smiling in spite of themselves, but they warn Bonza that he had better show up in court. Then, looking at you and Jeff, one of them says, "You kids had better be on your way home in a hurry, or you'll get a summons, too!"

You and Jeff say good-bye to Bonza. "Thanks for the magic show," you say.

"Anytime!" Bonza calls as you head down the walk.

Turn to page 93.

100

You can't believe it—the heavy ball is floating in midair! Then you almost kick yourself as you realize that you should be trying to figure out the trick. As you're thinking this, the lights dim a bit and take on a slightly reddish hue.

You can still see the ball clearly though as Bonza comes back onstage. "Here, I'll put the ball a little higher, where you can see it better," he says. He raises it about a foot and then leaves it again, still apparently floating in thin air.

At that moment the thought comes to you that the ball might be suspended by a tiny black thread, which would be virtually invisible against the black backdrop. Even so, you wonder how the thread could hold up such a heavy ball . . . unless the ball isn't as heavy as it looks.

Turn to page 63.

The cops have gotten into their car. The car's red flasher and siren start up as they wheel around and drive slowly toward the criminals. One cop has his rifle trained on them out the window.

The other officer says over his loudspeaker, *"Come out with your hands up!"*

Another siren sounds in the distance. The criminals must have heard it, too. The car doors open, and they come out, hands in the air.

Later a police officer gives you a ride home. You explain everything that happened, even how you and Jeff snuck into the Great Bonza's barn. The officer shakes his head in amazement.

"Bonza could prosecute you for trespassing," he says. "But I'm sure he won't. You saved him from being robbed, and you helped us catch two of the most wanted criminals in the state."

Turn to page 115.

"Stand over there with your back to the water," the gunman says, "We're going to make this look like a hunting accident."

You can't believe what's happening. Reluctantly you start to do as he says, but you're secretly thinking about which way to run after you set off the smoke bomb. You're pretty sure you can outrun the two men, but the clearing you're in is pretty wide—there's a good chance they'd have a clear shot at you before you could make it into the woods. A better idea crosses your mind. You haven't exactly learned to drive a car yet, but you know how one works. If you could start the engine and throw it into reverse before the smoke clears, you might be able to keep your head low and drive away.

There's no time to think anymore—in one swift motion you whip out the canister and set off the smoke bomb.

Within a split second a dense cloud of smoke surrounds the two men. You whirl around and jump into the front seat of the car. You don't even take time to close the door. The key's in the ignition—you turn it. The engine starts, but you were so rushed that you forgot to shift into reverse. The car surges toward the lake. You turn the wheel hard to the right. The open front door swings out, smacking the man with the deer rifle. The gun goes flying out of his hand and into the lake. But you and the car go into the lake, too!

Go on to the next page.

In a second, water is gurgling up over the hood. You dive out the window on the opposite side. You're a good swimmer, and you should be able to make it across the lake, but the water is freezing cold. You tread water and glance at the men onshore. The smoke has thinned out, but they're still coughing, sputtering, and rubbing their eyes. The smoke bomb worked well. Maybe you should just wade out and hide in the woods.

*If you try to make it across the lake,
turn to page 109.*

*If you wade out and try to hide in the woods,
turn to page 111.*

"I'd rather have the two hundred and fifty dollars," you say.

"Fine," says Bonza, "I'll mail a check to you today. You should have it by tomorrow. Tell your friend I'll call him later and see what he would like."

"Thanks very much."

"I'll give you a suggestion about what to do with the money," he says. "Put it in the bank where it will earn interest. By the time you're ready for college, it will have grown quite a bit. College is expensive, and it's wise to save as much money as possible ahead of time."

"Okay. Thanks again," you say. Right now college is the last thing you want to think about.

When Jeff calls you later, he tells you that he decided to take the money and buy himself a mountain bike. By the time Bonza's check comes the next day, you've decided that you'd really like to learn some great magic tricks. You spend half the reward money on magician's equipment and books. The rest you reluctantly put in the bank, as Bonza suggested.

You have a lot of fun with your magic set, but you don't seem to be getting very good at being a magician. I'll *never* become a master of magic like Bonza, you think. If only I could learn his biggest secret!

Turn to page 82.

Bonza returns in a moment without the ball and sits down on the edge of the stage with his legs dangling over the side.

"That was a great trick—how did you do it?" you ask.

He says, "You thought the ball might be suspended from above, didn't you?"

"Yes, but you proved it wasn't."

"If you're like most people," says Bonza, "you thought the ball was heavy because it looks heavy. Actually, it's very light. It's hollow, and the surface isn't steel, but the thinnest possible aluminum. You could dent it with your little finger. Secondly, you thought that if the ball *was* suspended on a thread, it would have to be from the top. However, since the ball is so light, it can be suspended from the sides." He beckons you up onstage and shows you how the threads ran from pulleys on each side of the stage. "That's why I could make a hoop with my arms and encircle the ball as I walked past it. If the ball had been suspended from above, my arm would have run into the thread, but since it was hung from the sides, my arms were encircling the supporting thread, too."

"But how did you make the ball move?"

"Another assumption you made," says Bonza, "is that you and I are alone . . . but, *presto* . . ." He looks over to the side of the stage. A woman walks out, and then a man comes on from the other side. "Meet my assistant, Gilda, and my cousin, Louis," says Bonza.

Turn to page 116.

In an angry voice, the driver says, "You could cause us trouble, all right—you've seen our faces."

You know that by this time Jeff will have called the local police. The entire force will be looking for you, and they'll have notified the state police, too. But that may not do you much good. Jeff has no description of the car, and no one driving by can see you squashed down on the floor.

"Slow down, Jake," the man in the back says. "We don't want to get pulled over for speeding."

"I get nervous on this highway," the driver replies. "Too many cars. How far to our turnoff for the river?"

"Four or five miles, on the right. It's just a narrow dirt road, but you can't miss it—it's exactly half a mile after Bob's Diner."

Turn to page 83.

You start swimming across the lake, stroking as hard as you can, hoping that the exercise will ward off the deadly chill that is creeping into your bones. You're a good swimmer, but the freezing water saps your strength. By the time you're half-way across the lake, you realize that you're not going to make it, and it's too late to turn back.

It would take some real magic to get you out of this one, you think. Unfortunately, that's your last thought. The cold water of the lake closes over your head.

The End

"I'd rather learn one of your secrets," you tell Bonza. After all, the knowledge of the Magic Master is something money can't buy!

"All right," says Bonza. "Stop by next Saturday morning at ten o'clock and I'll show you."

Jeff decides to take the money. When Saturday rolls around, you arrive at Bonza's house alone. He invites you into a room that looks like a small theater. There is a stage at one end of the room, with several rows of chairs facing it. There's no curtain across the front of the stage, but a black backdrop hangs across the rear.

"Sit wherever you'd like," Bonza says.

You choose a seat in the middle of the second row. Bonza leaps onto the stage and then disappears off to one side. He returns a moment later holding a large silver ball about the size of a basketball. It looks as if it's made of steel and is obviously quite heavy.

"Now I'll show you a trick," Bonza says. He holds up a finger, as if to emphasize what he's saying.

"I'm ready when you are," you say.

"When a show begins," says Bonza, "it's customary to dim the lights a little." Saying that, he leaves the ball floating in the air and walks offstage.

Turn to page 100.

You wade quickly to shore and climb out on the bank. The man who lost his rifle has no other weapon, but the second man has a revolver, and it's pointed right at you. You race into the woods as a bullet whistles past your ear. Then you dodge through the trees, darting right and left. Another shot hits a tree so close that it splits off a piece of bark that cuts your cheek. You don't care—that's one bullet less in the man's gun.

More shots follow, but they seem farther away. You keep your eyes low, making sure you don't trip, and you don't slow down until you're completely out of breath. Then you stop and listen, and hear nothing but the whispering of the wind in the trees.

You jog on through the woods, worrying about whether you'll be lost all night, and whether the robbers are tracking you. Then, ahead, you see a welcome sight—the back of Bob's Diner. You burst in the kitchen door, yelling, "Call the police!"

A month has passed, and you're as happy as can be. The police quickly caught the gunmen. It turned out that your captors were escaped bank robbers. As a reward, the Great Bonza has given you a job as his assistant and you have learned some of his most amazing tricks. At school you're famous. Other kids are practically asking for your autograph. And why not? Not many of them could outwit two of the most wanted criminals in the state.

The End

"Objection!" Mr. Kramer says loudly. "The witness is not qualified to know whether the witness is a magician or not."

"Your Honor," says Mr. Stafford, "the witness's belief is relevant to the issue here."

"Objection overruled," says the judge. "Answer the question."

"I guess I'm getting to be a pretty good magician," you say.

"Now, do you think you know the difference between something that's legal and something that's illegal?" Mr. Stafford asks.

"Yes," you say.

"So you would know if something you were doing were illegal?"

"Yes, I think so."

"All right. Now do the tricks you've learned so far involve anything illegal?" the lawyer asks.

"No, they don't," you reply.

"Very good, very good," says Mr. Stafford. He walks away from you and faces the jury. "That's as it should be, isn't it? There's nothing wrong with a magic trick when there's nothing harmful or illegal about it." He whirls around and strides back toward you. "But tell me, as a young magician, can you think of a reasonable explanation for a man on a horse disappearing into thin air?"

Turn to page 76.

114

It won't do you much good to foil the criminals if it means you'll get killed in a car accident. You decide to keep still and wait for a better opportunity.

A moment later the car brakes, turns sharply, then accelerates again. You figure that the driver has turned down the dirt road. After another minute or so the car slows to a stop.

The man who has been holding you down says, "Stay there until we tell you." You watch out of the corner of your eye as he gets out. The driver also gets out, and the two of them stand by the car whispering. You have a sinking feeling that they're trying to decide how to kill you.

"Okay, kid, come on out—on this side," one of them says.

You put your elbows on the backseat as you raise yourself up from the floor, then twist around to get out of the car. While your back is to the men, you reach in your pocket and feel the red button on top of the smoke bomb.

As you get out of the car, you have only a second to look around. The car is parked in a broad, grassy area at the end of a dirt road. The front of the car is only a few yards from the edge of a lake. The lake is surrounded by dense woods, except for a few cabins on the far side.

You plant a foot on the ground. One of the men is holding a deer rifle. You hear a click as he takes off the safety catch.

Turn to page 102.

The next day you get a call from the Great Bonza. "I'd like to scold you for sneaking into my barn," he says. "But even more, I'd like to thank you for being so quick-witted and foiling those robbers."

"I'm sure glad that smoke bomb worked," you say. "Without it, I would have been a goner."

"I'd like to give you and your friend each a reward of two hundred and fifty dollars," Bonza says.

"Hey, thanks!"

Bonza pauses for a moment, then continues thoughtfully. "In fact, you did such a great job that I'm going to let you choose your own reward. You can have the money, or if you prefer, I'll teach you one of my important secrets."

You think for a moment, wondering whether learning one of Bonza's secrets would be worth more than two hundred and fifty dollars. After all, he is the Magic Master.

*If you say you'll take the money,
turn to page 104.*

*If you say you'd rather learn Bonza's secret,
turn to page 110.*

Bonza continues, "This trick is not my most elaborate by any means, but it illustrates my greatest secret perfectly."

"What is your greatest secret?" you say curiously.

"To understand my greatest secret, you must understand this," says the magician. "Things are not always what they seem to be. Things don't always happen the way we think they happen. We all make assumptions about things without realizing it. You assumed that the ball was too heavy to be suspended by a thread. You also assumed that I had no assistants. Nearly everyone would make the same assumptions. And so . . ."

"Yes?" You lean forward eagerly.

"People tend to think that things can't happen except in a particular way. If I can make something happen in another way—one that people wouldn't normally think of—then they'll think it must have happened by magic."

"Gosh."

"That one simple idea is the basis for nearly every trick," Bonza says. "And now that you know it, I'm going to give you something if you'll promise to keep it a secret. Does that sound fair?"

"Sure," you say. "But what?"

"Two hundred and fifty dollars," says Bonza, smiling.

The End

ABOUT THE AUTHOR

EDWARD PACKARD is a graduate of Princeton University and Columbia Law School. He developed the unique storytelling approach used in the Choose Your Own Adventure series while thinking up stories for his children, Caroline, Andrea, and Wells.

ABOUT THE ILLUSTRATOR

FRANK BOLLE studied at Pratt Institute. He has worked as an illustrator for many national magazines and now creates and draws cartoons for magazines as well. He has also worked in advertising and children's educational materials and has drawn and collaborated on several newspaper comic strips, including *Annie* and *Winnie Winkle*. He has illustrated many books in the Choose Your Own Adventure series, including *Master of Kung Fu, South Pole Sabotage, Return of the Ninja, You Are a Genius, Through the Black Hole, The Worst Day of Your Life, Master of Tae Kwon Do, The Cobra Connection, Hijacked!, Master of Karate, Invaders From Within, The Lost Ninja, Daredevil Park, Kidnapped!, The Terrorist Trap,* and *Ghost Train.* A native of Brooklyn Heights, New York, Mr. Bolle now lives and works in Westport, Connecticut.

A CHOOSE YOUR OWN ADVENTURE® BOOK

PASSPORT

THE NEWS TEAM THAT COVERS THE WORLD

YOU MAKE THE NEWS!

You are an anchor for the Passport news team.
Together with Jake, your cameraman, and Eddy, an
investigative journalist, you travel the world on assignment,
covering firsthand some of the hottest events in the news.